Teacher's pet

Story by Carole Mohr

Illustrations by Mark Weber

Dr. Judith Nadell, Series Editor

It was Nicole's first day in Mrs. Hall's class.

Mrs. Hall said everyone should make Nicole feel welcome.

During art, Mrs. Hall picked Nicole to pass out the markers.

This made Sara mad.

She wanted to pass out the markers.

Mrs. Hall said she liked Nicole's drawing.

This also made Sara mad.

Soon it was time for recess.

"Don't play with Nicole," said Sara

to the girls.

"She's the teacher's pet, and she stinks."

Nicole went over to the girls.

"Does anyone want to play kickball?"

she asked.

Nobody wanted to play.

Emily saw how sad Nicole looked.

She was all alone with the kickball.

Emily knew Nicole did not feel welcome.

"Nicole does **not** stink," Emily said to herself.

"She is **not** the teacher's pet.

She seems nice."

"I'll play with you," Emily said to Nicole.

"We'll have fun."

"Can we play, too?" asked Jasmin and Kendra.

If you were Nicole, what would **you** say?